Alphabetical Soup

written and illustrated by
Suzy Spafford

BORIS'S RIVER SERVICE

WHEN you're really good-and-hungry,
and feeling a little adventurous,
a great place to go for lunch
is down the River Wanda Meander
to Dooley's Diner in the Murky Marsh.

Copyright ©1995 Suzy Spafford
Suzy's Zoo, San Diego, California 92121
All rights reserved
Printed in Mexico
Second Printing, July 1995

Illustrations created
in transparent color markers
with colored pencil enhancement

AND ONE DAY, when the three very good friends, Suzy Ducken, Jack Quacker and Corky Turtle were starting to think about lunch, and were feeling a little adventurous, that is just exactly what they did.

Now, Dooley Stegasouposaurus and his helper, Sammy Frog, run a most unusual diner, serve very different food, and are known far and wide for odd-but-tasty specials.

That day's offering was a steamy bowl of Murky Marsh Mush, with a cool glass of Honeysuckle Punch, followed by a frosty Magnolia Marshcicle for dessert.

Jack and Corky generally stay pretty quiet while they eat, but Suzy loves to chatter and ask questions.

"What's the very best special you've ever made?" she asked Dooley as she slurped up the last of her punch with a straw.

"Why, my grandmother's recipe for 'Alphabetical Soup,'" he replied without hesitation.

"You mean, *alphabet* soup—the kind that has little letters in it?" said Corky between mouthfuls of mush.

A B C D E F G H I J K L M

"Nope, this is *Alphabetical* Soup. You start with 'A' and go all the way to 'Z,' adding something good to eat for every letter of the alphabet. If you make it correctly, it's delicious and nutritious, guaranteed!"

"Can you add mustard and chocolate syrup?" asked Corky.

"And ketchup?" added Jack.

"Yuck!" said Suzy, as she wrinkled her beak.

"Why, that's a very tasty combo," replied Dooley. "But if you don't go in alphabetical order, weird things can happen. First, the soup will fizzle and burp...

...and then roil and boil, and then turn into goo, and...

EXPLODE!

It's happened before," he explained meekly.

"I'm sure we can help you stay in alphabetical order," offered Corky.
"You think so? Let's see... a-p-c-d-e-f-b... then r-i-j-k... uh... m-n-l-o-p... " stammered Dooley. "Well, I do get confused. There are so many letters."

The three friends looked at each other and Suzy rolled her eyes. Jack said, "Boy! I sure can see how the soup might explode sometimes!"

"Saaay! I'll bet we could make Alphabetical Soup with their help, Sammy!" exclaimed Dooley. And they all nodded excitedly.

N O P Q R S T U V W X Y Z

"**S**pread the word! Invite everyone to come! We'll all make Alphabetical Soup…

…guaranteed delicious and nutritious," called out Dooley as he and Sammy waved them good-bye.

Come to DOOLEY'S DINER
in the Murky Marsh
for
Alphabetical Soup!
Everybody bring
something to put
in it!
We need good stuff
for EVERY LETTER.
Sign Up!

Bring your food thing and
meet at 10:00 a.m. Saturday
at Boris's Ferry Landing!

Sign-Up List
Name
Food
Letter

Back at Suzy's house, the three friends busily made posters inviting everyone to come.

By Saturday morning quite a crowd had gathered at Boris Apatosaurus's ferry, with wonderful things for the soup. Everyone chattered happily, and looked to see what the others had brought.

Soon all were safely buckled onto Boris's back. Then they noisily made their way down the Wanda Meander to Dooley's Diner in the Murky Marsh.

"Welcome, friends," greeted Dooley. "Did you all remember to come hungry?"

They had everything ready. The picnic tables were covered with checkered cloths. Soup bowls in every color were stacked high, and all the spoons were polished and twinkling.

Suzy wrote down all the letters in perfect alphabetical order. Everyone started to gather around the soup pot, eager for their food letter to be called.

"Let the Soup begin!" declared Dooley.

"A," said Suzy. "That's first."
"Applesauce," said Emily Marmot.
"And asparagus,"
added Tillamook Mouse.
"All-righty," said Dooley.
"You both get A-plus."

"B," called Suzy.
"Broccoli broth by the bucket,"
said Livingston Elephant.
"And blueberries, fresh-picked
this morning," added Sally Ducken.

"Beautiful!"
exclaimed Dooley.
Sammy stirred as the
berries bobbed around
in the broth.

"'C' is next," called Suzy.

"That's us," chorused Corinne Turtle and her cooking class. "We've brought cabbage and carrots, catsup and celery."

"Did you mention 'ketchup'?" asked Dooley. "Doesn't that start with 'k'?"

"Says here you can spell it either way," answered Corky.

"We brought corn!" chirped Clara's brood of chicks. "Cool," said Dooley.

Then Suzy called for 'D.'

"A dozen donuts," said Davy Raccoon.

"Delightful!" declared Dooley.

"Hey, Dooley!" came a wispy little voice from down by Dooley's foot. "How about nice, fresh dirt?"

"Oh, it's *you*, Eli. Sorry, little friend, dirt is not good to eat."

"E," said Suzy. "Elwood, you look sad," said Dooley.

"I couldn't find anything for 'E,'" explained Elwood Marmot.

"I got an idea," exclaimed Davy. "How about eggs?"

GASP!

Aw, Eli... don't give up!

"NO!" shrieked Clara.

"How DARE you!" she huffed.

Hmpff!

Peep!

"What about eggplant, or endive, or escarole?" suggested Corky.

"Wait!" said Elwood happily. "I remembered! I have elderberries in my pocket. You may have them both. Is that enough?"

"Definitely, lad," said Dooley.

"F," called out Suzy.

Fritz Fox said, "I brought french fries. I have fifteen left... uh... I guess maybe now there are fourteen."

"I brought fiddlehead fern shoots, and they're fresh-picked from the forest," said Hazel Squirrel.

You ever eat fern shoots?

Yes! They're fabulous fricasee'd with fennel!

"Grandma Gussie, 'G' is next. What did you bring?"

"Grits, child—grits and gravy, your favorite."

"Mm-mm-mmmm!" murmured the crowd. It was everybody's very favorite food, too.

"H," Suzy called next.

"Hey, Hugo, better hurry. Stanley's and Rory's ice cream is dripping."

Hugo Bear held out his hat and said, "Honey from a hive in a hickory tree behind my hou-OUCH!"

An angry bee stung Hugo on the ear. He bumped Rory Tiger, and ice cream slid into the soup. So did the hat full of honey.

"I-yi-yi!" gasped Suzy. "Both 'H' and 'I' went in at the same time! Is the soup OK?"

As they peered into the pot, it burped a single lonely little bubble, and everyone let out a sigh of relief.

"Now 'J,'" said Suzy. "I brought jalapeños. We jackrabbits love 'em. But be careful—they're hot!" warned Jennifer.

"We like hot. Go ahead, Sammy you try one too," said Dooley.

"Gaaahh!"

they howled.

"Here—quick! Jicama juice is just what you need," offered Jason.

"Whew! Let's put in *just one* jalapeño, Sammy!" advised Dooley.

"You OK?" asked Suzy.
"Whew! OK," replied Dooley.
"Then 'K' is next," said Suzy.

"One kohlrabi," said Kirsten Kangaroo.
"I always wondered what those weird things were," said Dooley.
"And young Kenneth is giving you a kiwi—his favorite," she added.
Then Kiley Koala handed up his basket of little orangey kumquats.

"We never knew there were so many different things to eat," said Suzy.

A Applesauce
   Asparagus
B Blueberries
   Broccoli Broth
C Cabbage
   Carrots
   Catsup
   Celery
   Corn
D Donuts
E Elderberries
F Fiddlehead
   Fern
   French fr
G Gravy
   grits
H Honey
I Ice Cream
J Jalapeños
   Jicama Juice
K Kiwi fruit
   Kohlrabi
   Ku
Q
R
S
T
U
V
W
X
Y

"Look who's got 'L.' It's my dad Lester and my little brother Chuckie and his pet frog Ribert." mama Lizzie and

"We've brought leeks, a lemon, lentils, and loquats," said Mrs. Ducken.
"Luscious!" exclaimed Dooley.

"And here with 'M' are Ollie and Martha Marmot."

"Martha brought mushrooms, and I brought mustard. That's right—give it a big squeeze, Sammy."

Hnnggh!

WHAT's all this muttering?!

MUD! MUD!

"'N' is next," called Suzy.
"Noodles," said Norm Egret. "What's soup without noodles?"

Oops! Not all of the noodles went into the soup!

"I brought olives for 'O.' That's next,
isn't it, Suzy?" asked Ollie, Jr.
"Of course," she said.

"Oh boy!
Oscar Otter has
brought onions—just
what a really good
soup needs," added
Dooley.

Meanwhile in Mr. Mudd's general store, Penelope Porcupine was gathering as many 'P' foods as she could carry. Her twin Quincy was searching for anything beginning with 'Q.' Jack found him a quart of quinces.

But suddenly, Quincy had an idea, and asked Mr. Mudd, "Do you have any q-cumbers?"

Mr. Mudd replied, "Cucumbers? Sure, my boy, right over there."

After paying for their selections, Penelope and Quincy dashed back to the soup.

"'P,' please," said Suzy. Penelope tossed in the parsnips, pears, peas, plums and one potato. She was very pleased with herself.

"Are you getting all that, Suzy?" asked Dooley.

"Not quite," she answered, as Corky helped her with the spelling.

"Ready for 'Q'?" asked Quincy. 'Cause *I* am, and here it is— a *q-cumber*," he said proudly, as he tossed it in.

"Corky, how do you spell *cucumber*?" asked Suzy.

"C-u-c…wait a minute…oh, no! Cucumber begins with 'C,' not '*Q*'!"

GASP!

"STOP!"

"Huh?" said Quincy.

The soup began to fizzle and burp, and the pot began to tremble. Then it roiled and boiled and Sammy was furiously flung round and round.

BONG!

The pot whanged down hard on the stove and Sammy was tossed into the air!

Then in one rumbling whoosh—

FROOOOM!

—the soup EXPLODED
twenty-six feet straight up
out of the pot!
   As it collected in a mass
of mottled goo, Jack streaked up
just as fast as he could
with Quincy's quart of quinces...

...and made a mighty jump up, sloshing them right into the middle of the soup... which quivered for a second, then whooshed back down into the pot in one giant SCHLOOP!...

...every single drop.

plook!

The soup pot hiccuped,

growled,

Hic!

Grrrrr...!

P-tooie!

THODK!

Eep!

and spit out the cucumber...

which burned a hole in the ground three feet deep!

"HURRAY! HURRAY!"
they all shouted.

Everyone was happy, except for Quincy,
who was so embarrassed that he ran away to hide.

"WOW!" said Suzy. "Alphabetical Soup is amazing! What do you think it tastes like *now*, Dooley?"

"We can't taste it yet," cautioned Dooley.
"You don't dare taste it until it's finished," he explained, as he put his tasting spoon back on his head.

A very unusual aroma began to lift and drift around the Murky Marsh. And by now everyone was becoming *really* good-and-hungry.

"Let's have the next letter," called Dooley.

"R," said Suzy.

"Right here," said Ritz Quacker and Randy Treerat.
Ritz had raisins and rice in his wagon.
Randy had a big, fat, juicy rutabaga he had pulled all by himself.

"And for 'S' it's Simon and Solly, Sammy's siblings, bringing sage and sassafras leaves. *Sniff! Sniff!* They sure smell good!" said Dooley.

"Time for 'T,'" said Suzy.
"It's Trudy Turkey and Thelma Turtle with tomatoes and turnips," said Dooley.

TURF WITH TOPSOIL!

Suzy called for 'U' next. "Yoo-hoo! It's me," chirped Cornelia Ostrich. "I brought the last piece of upside-down cake…

…left over from my umpty-umth birthday."

"Why, it's Violet Rabbit with things for 'V'!"
"Yes," she said, in her very soft voice.
"I brought a drop of vanilla, and
a splash of vinegar."

"W," called Jack this time. "We're getting close,
and I'm starving!"
"Water!" said Graham Quacker.
What a relief! The soup
had become very hard
to stir.

OH, WOE!

aww, Eli!

"Dooley, we're at 'X,' and I don't think anybody brought anything," said Suzy, sounding worrie[d]. "Ah! I have exactly the thing for 'X' right here," he replied, as he reached behind the board.

"It's my grandmother's extraordinary xylophone, made from extra branches of the near-extinct xanthan tree. It gives off an excellent extract," he explained.

"We'll steep it in the soup for exactly 'X' minutes. That's Roman for ten, you know."

"Pretty magical, Dooley!" exclaimed Suzy.

"Y," called Corky.
"Your turn, Herkimer," said Dooley, "and that's a mighty big carton."
"It's yam yogurt, freshly made yesterday," puffed Herkimer Mouse.
"How yummy!" said Dooley.

"We made it to 'Z,'" called Suzy.
"Whee!" cheered everyone.

"Zounds! What's that, D.J.?" gasped Dooley.
"A monster zucchini," said D.J. Ducken.

"What a great way to finish the soup," remarked Dooley. Sammy wondered how it would ever fit into the pot.

The chart on the sign reads:

A Applesauce Asparagus
B Blueberries Broccoli Broth
C Cabbage Carrots Catsup Celery Corn
D Donuts
E Elderberries
F Fiddlehead Ferns French Fries
G Gravy & grits
H Honey
I Ice Cream
J Jalapeño pepper Jicama Juice
K Kiwi Kohlrabi Kumquats
L Leeks Lemon lentils loquat
M Mushrooms mustard
N Noodles
O Olives Onions
P Parsnip peas pear plums potato
Q Quince
R Raisins rice
S Sage Sassafrass
T Tomatoes Turnip
U Upside-down cake
V Vanilla vinegar
W Water
X Xylophone of Xanthan Wood
Y Yam Yogurt
Z Zucchini

Yaaay! We did it!

After the huge zucchini was eased into the soup, the aroma started changing. It tingled and prickled its way into everyone's nostrils. Quincy abandoned his hiding place, and even Mr. Mudd was lured out of his store.

Dooley helped Sammy stir. The soup gently bubbled and brewed, making juicy little blooping sounds.

"Is it time to taste it yet?" Suzy asked.

"Yes. It is time," Dooley replied, dipping his tasting spoon into the pot.

SSzzipp! Dooley tasted while everyone watched hungrily. "Hmmm… " he said slowly.

"Tell us! Tell us! Is it delicious? You guaranteed it would be! Is it? Is it?"

they all asked, everyone talking at once and pressing closer with their bowls.

"First, you should tell us what *you* think, Suzy," he said.

She dipped her spoon into the colorful broth and carefully blew on the steaming mouthful.

All eyes fastened upon her as she delicately took a sip. And just as the flavor of the soup reached the back of her tongue,

"ZOWIE!"

"De-e-licious!"

she raved, as she rose three feet up off the bench.

Soon, everyone was agreeing heartily, as they gobbled up bowl after bowl of Alphabetical Soup.

"It was the rutabaga that made it delicious," came a voice from the group. "No way, the jalapeño did it….How about my kumquats?…The xylophone! The xylophone!" The opinions and comments continued for quite awhile.

Finally Jack asked, "How did you know it would be so delicious, Dooley?

"That's easy. It was all of you who made the soup delicious, because *everyone* helped, and you were *really* good-and-hungry!" he explained.

"Hey!—and it was fun! Let's make it again!" shouted Rory.

There was a pause. Then, "Yes! *Yes! YES!*" cheered the group. And soon they were laughing and burping and giggling and chattering and planning another whole batch.

So, what unusual things do you suppose these good friends will bring, next time they go down to the Murky Marsh, to make this delicious… nutritious… and magical soup?